WILDEST COWBOY

For my darling Asa ~ G.J.

For Lisa. Stay wild! ~ S.O.

First published 2017 by Macmillan Children's Books
This edition published 2018 by Macmillan Children's Books
an imprint of Pan Macmillan
20 New Wharf Road, London N1 9RR
Associated companies throughout the world
www.panmacmillan.com

ISBN 978-1-4472-3147-9

A CIP catalogue record for this book
is available from the British Library.

Printed in China

Written by
Garth Jennings

Illustrated by
Sara Ogilvie

The Wildest Cowboy

MACMILLAN CHILDREN'S BOOKS

Way out in the West there's a town they call Fear,
And only the roughest and toughest live here.
They never eat treats for they'd sooner chew rocks,
And inside their boots they wear rattlesnake socks.

They spit and they sneer and they snarl all the time,
And they comb out their nits with a live porcupine!
Even the vultures are scared to fly near
The wild folks that live in the town they call Fear.

But one day a stranger rolled into town.
A colourful fellow named Bingo B. Brown!
From the spring in his step to the size of his grin,
It was clear that in Fear he would never fit in.

His little dog danced as he started to sing,

"Roll up!
Roll up!

Come see what I bring!"

"I have boomerang hats!

I have waterproof suits!

Elastic lassos and inflatable boots!

I have braces and laces you play like a bassist,
And bow ties that flap to keep flies off your faces!

I have treats by the ton,

I have goodies galore!

Roll up! Roll up!

For the WILDEST store!"

But the townsfolk were silent. Not a word or a sigh.
Just the rustle of tumbleweed tumbling by.

"Where's all the happiness? Where's all the joy?"
Asked Bingo B. Brown of a small, nervous boy.

The little boy whispered, "Now listen here stranger.
You and your dog are in terrible danger.
For when the sun sets and the night starts to fall,
A cowboy comes calling who's wildest of all!"

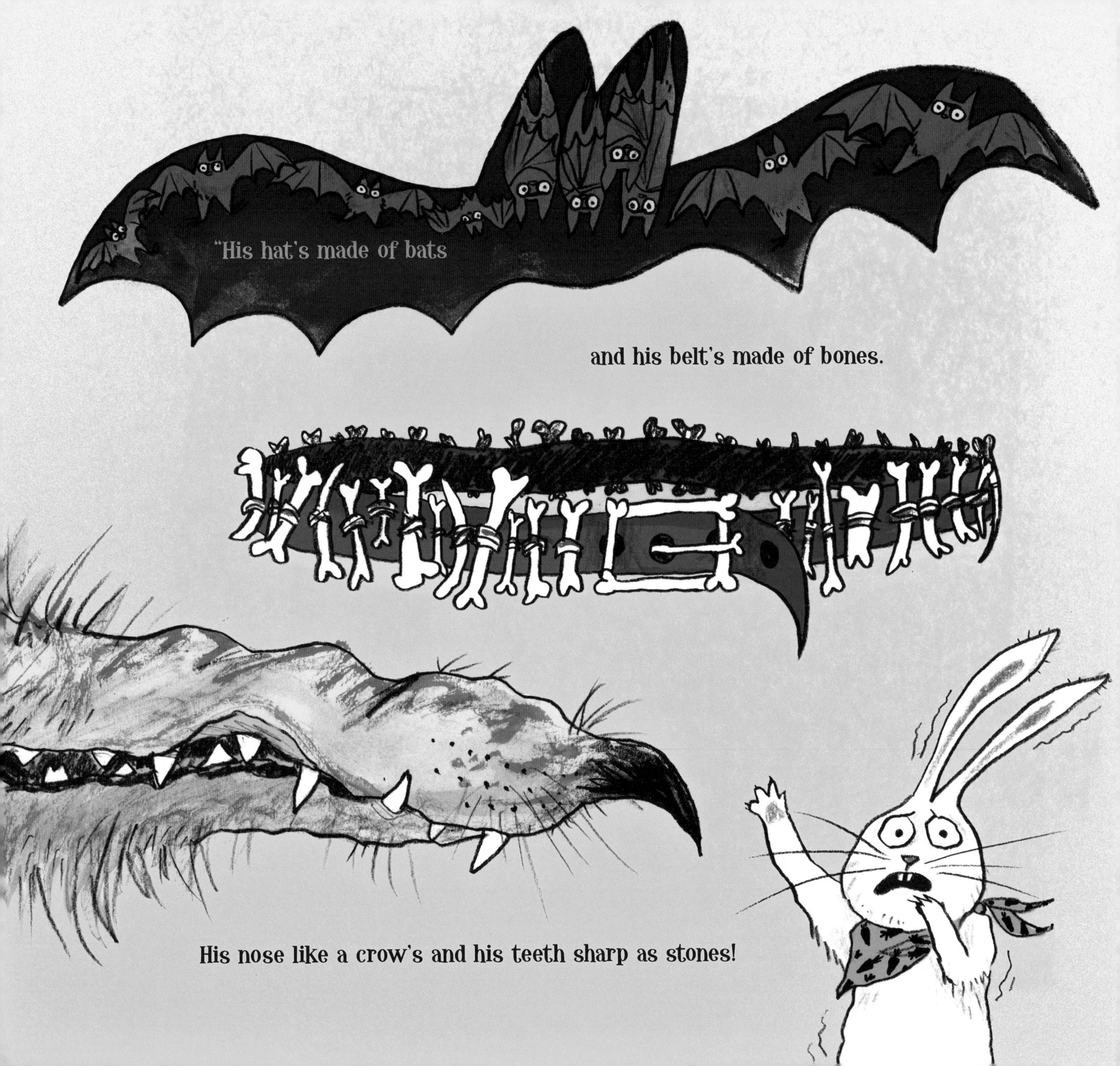

"His hat's made of bats

and his belt's made of bones.

His nose like a crow's and his teeth sharp as stones!

His laugh is like thunder,
His horse moves like lightning.
We all live in fear for we all find him

frightening!"

Bingo was scared and his dog felt the same,
So they packed up their stall and they caught the next train.

"Sorry to dash but we really can't stay!" Called Bingo B. Brown as the train chuffed away.

"What a relief! But – oh! What a sad town.
I feel bad for them all," sighed Bingo B. Brown.
But all was not right. The dog heard a sound . . .
Could it be thundering hooves on the ground?

And a hat made of bats and a belt made of bones.
A nose like a crow's and those teeth sharp as stones.
His laugh was like thunder, his horse fast as lightning.
The townsfolk were right – he was ever so frightening!

Just like a frog the beast leaped from his ride,
Burst through the window and landed inside!

"Ha ha!" Roared the cowboy, "I'm here to spread fear.
All knees should be knocking whenever I'm near!"
"Please stop!" shouted Bingo. "This just isn't fair!"
But the cowboy hurled Bingo right up through the air.

Up, up he shot, like a streak through the sky,
Where he landed (what luck!) on a vulture nearby.
"Please help me," begged Bingo, "and follow that track.
My dog's on that train and I must get him back!"

They flew through the canyon and under the bridge.
They darted through dustbowls and swooped round the ridge.

Inside the train the dog trembled with fear.
He thought to himself, "I wish Bingo was here."

Now it's not all that often that wishes come true,
But suddenly, in through the window he flew!

"Hey cowboy," cried Bingo. "I'm not here to fight
But you're scaring my dog and that just isn't right!
Quite frankly we've had all the fear we can take.
It's time that you stopped, so I'm pulling the brake!"

Screeeeeech went the brakes and "OUCH" came the sound
As the cowboy fell flat with a SPLAT on the ground.
Out burst the bow ties, the treats and the boots.
The braces, the laces and waterproof suits.

And just as a rolling wave washes the shore,
The cowboy was covered in goodies galore.
They washed all the wicked right out of his head,
And left him quite calm and quite happy instead.

As the train chuffed and puffed its way back into town,
The cowboy just listened to Bingo B. Brown.
He learned of the terror and fear he had spread,
And how folks prefer laughing and joking instead.

The cowboy was grateful — at last he could see.
"Just wait 'till those folks get to meet the new me!"

But the townsfolk were silent. Not a word or a sigh.
Then the little boy whispered, "Hey, who IS this guy?"

The little dog danced and then Bingo joined in,
As the cowboy jumped up and he started to sing . . .

"Hello, I'm Frank and I've come back to say,
That thanks to these fellas I've found a new way.
I'll no longer scare you — I'll never be spiteful.
I promise, from now, I'll be simply delightful!"

From miles around you could hear the loud cheer,
Of all the poor folks who'd been living in Fear.
And ever since then the town's not been the same.
It's different in many ways, even its name.

They called the town Hope and they built a new store,
Where the little dog dances and Frank sweeps the floor.
"Roll up! Roll up!" calls Bingo each day,
And the folks they just love it, they can't stay away!

You see, living in Hope is much nicer than Fear.
You must come and visit, you're all welcome here.
From the songs that we sing to the way we are dressed,
We're the wildest cowboys in all of the West!